TEMPTED BY MY ROOMMATE

SHAW HART

 Created with Vellum

WANT A FREE BOOK?

***You can grab Sweets* Here.**
**Check out my website, www.shawhart.com for
more free books!**

*

Falling for him would be a mistake.

Rae Mitchell has never been in love. She's never even been in like. The boys in high school didn't do anything for her and she was starting to think that there was something wrong with her.

Then she meets him.

Brooks Coleman.

He's everything that she wants — Tall, tatted, charming. He's even a freaking war hero.

There's just one problem.

He's her new roommate and she doesn't need to be an expert at love to know that starting something with him right now might not be the best idea.

He's just so tempting though...

ONE

Rae

"I CAN'T BELIEVE that you're leaving me," I say dramatically as Palmer sets the last of her boxes down.

"I'm right next door," she says with a laugh and I sigh.

"I know, but things are going to be so different now."

"We'll still see each other all the time. We can ride together on the days that we have the same classes," she assures me, and I sigh again.

"I know, but now you're living with a guy. It's going to change things. You'll be too busy with Banks to spend time with me."

"We'll still have girl's nights. Don't forget, you're living with a guy now too."

I look over to the wall, knowing that Brooks is moving into Palmer's old room as we speak.

"It's weird." I pout and she laughs.

"It won't be. Brooks is really nice and he seems to keep

to himself. It will be like you have the whole place to yourself."

I want to tell Palmer that that's not the reason why I'm kind of freaking out. Sure, I'm going to miss living with her, but she's right next door and we'll see each other all the time.

The problem is that I don't know if I can live with Brooks and keep my hands to myself.

An image of his perfect face fills my head and I bite my bottom lip as I lean against the bedroom wall. He's got dark brown hair that's still cropped close to his head from his military days. Even though it's still pretty short, I still want to run my fingers through it.

That's not what gets me though. It's his eyes. He's got these piercing blue eyes and every time he looks at me, I swear that he can see right through me.

The first time that I met him, I tried to convince myself that I was just unnerved by him and that's why shivers ran down my spine whenever I was close to him.

Then the dreams started happening, and I couldn't lie to myself anymore.

I have a crush on the guy.

And now he's going to be my roommate.

"Are you working tonight?" Palmer asks and I shake my head.

"No, I have it off. I'm not on again until tomorrow."

"Bummer. I have tomorrow off."

"We both work Saturday," I point out and she smiles.

"Look at us making plans to see each other already."

I roll my eyes at her and she grins.

"I'll let you guys get settled," I say as Palmer's boyfriend comes into the bedroom.

"See you later!" Palmer calls and I don't look back because I'm sure that they're already kissing.

I'm happy for my friend. She deserves to be happy and Banks definitely makes her that. He'd walk through fire for her if it made her smile.

I just wish that I could have that too.

I flinch at that thought. I know that my mother would lose her mind if she knew that I was thinking about settling down with the enemy.

I love my mom, but she's a difficult woman to care for. She has such high morals and if you mess up once, you're done. She doesn't give second chances and she expects me to be the same. I have a feeling that she's going to want me to move back in with her after I graduate and I'm not looking to our version of Grey Gardens.

My parents divorced when I was fourteen. My dad had drunkenly kissed another woman, or rather she kissed him and according to my mom, he didn't react fast enough to push her away. That was the beginning of the end for them. He apologized and begged for forgiveness, but my mom never accepted. She said that she couldn't trust him.

Sometimes I think that she was looking for a way out where she wouldn't be the bad guy, and she jumped when the kissing thing happened.

She tried to get me to hate my dad after that, but I never could. Everyone makes mistakes and while I don't know how I would feel if my spouse did something similar, I feel like I would have tried couples counseling or something before I jumped to divorce. I mean, he didn't even kiss her back and it wasn't like he went after her.

My dad died a few years ago. He never remarried or even dated after the divorce and I know that he still loved my mom and me, even if she didn't let me see him as much as I would have liked once they split.

Now she's all the family that I have left.

"How's it going?" I ask Gray as I head into my apartment.

"Good, we've got all of the boxes in his room," he tells me, wiping some sweat from his forehead.

"Want me to order some pizza or something?" I offer, but he shakes his head.

"I'm going to get home to Nora and the pups," he says as he digs his phone out of his pocket.

"Oh, okay. Tell her I said hi."

"Will do," he says. "I'll see you later, Brooks!"

"See ya! Thanks again," my new roommate calls back and I watch Gray go, wondering if I should make the same offer of pizza to Brooks.

I walk closer to the open bedroom doorway and peek in. He's busy putting some of the boxes away, and I step closer.

"Need a hand?" I ask and he looks over at me.

Those blue eyes meet mine and I stop breathing.

"No, I got it."

He looks back to the box at his feet and I take a deep breath.

"I was going to order pizza. Do you want anything?"

"No, I'm going out to meet Ender here in a few. Thanks though."

I stand there awkwardly for a minute, watching him unpack before I turn and head down the short hallway to my own room. I'm right next door to him and the bathroom is just past my room at the end of the hallway.

My stomach growls, reminding me that I skipped lunch because I was running late to my afternoon class and I pull my phone out of my pocket and pull up my favorite pizza place's menu.

I hear the front door open and close as I place my order and I don't know why that makes me so sad. It's probably for the best that I don't spend that much time with Brooks. It seems like every time I'm around him, I fall for him a little more.

Everyone agrees that he's a good guy. He gets along with everyone from Eye Candy Ink and gives good advice. At least he did to Banks because that's why he pulled his head out of his butt and went after Palmer when he thought that he was too old for her.

He's kind and patient with everyone and is always willing to help out, even though he's still healing from his injuries.

I wonder what he thinks of me.

I put on my pajamas and answer the door when my pizza is delivered. As I grab a slice and curl up on the couch, I wonder if this is the life that I want.

Is my mother doing the same thing right now? Is she happy?

Somehow, I doubt it. I actually can't remember the last time that I saw her smile or laugh. I've been trying to live up to her standards since I was a kid and I know that she's happy that I've never brought around a guy or dated, but is that what I really want? Or am I just trying to live my life to make my mother proud of me?

I think I know the answer to that question and I take a big bite of my pizza so that I don't have to think about it.

I shouldn't even worry about any of this. Brooks is the first man that has ever made me want a relationship or anything more and I don't think that he's interested in me.

Besides, he's going to be my roommate for the foreseeable future so I shouldn't get too worked up on this.

It's just a silly crush. I'm sure that it will pass soon.

That thought feels like a lie though, so I grab the remote and try to drown out my thoughts.

TWO

Brooks

I'M early to meet Ender but I had to get out of the apartment. Being around Rae is torture.

She's so sweet and she looks so soft. Every time I see her, I just want to grab her and kiss her but I don't think that she would like that. I can just picture her rejecting me, looking at me like I'm insane, and then I spend the rest of my life trying to avoid her.

I think I should try to start this roommate thing off on a better foot than that.

My shoulder is killing me after moving boxes and clothes for most of the afternoon. I'm lucky that Niall stopped by. The other guys at Eye Candy Ink offered to help too but they all worked today and I didn't want to wait until the shop closed to start.

My phone rings as I rub my shoulder and I wonder if I should cancel on Ender and go home to ice it. I check the screen and smile slightly when I see that it's my friend Jasper calling me.

"Miss me already?" I joke as I answer it.

"Not at all," he deadpans back and I laugh.

I stayed with Jasper when I first got back to the States. He was back in Rosewood, Colorado, for his father's funeral and I stayed for a couple days to help him get his house ready to sell. Jasper and I were both trying to figure out what to do now that we were out of the military.

Jasper ended up staying in Rosewood with his now-fiancée, Evangeline, while I came up to Pittsburgh for a change of pace.

So far, I like it more than the small-town life, but I still don't know what I want to do with the rest of my life.

I've been working out at King's Gym with a few friends and trying to get my shoulder and left side back to a hundred percent. I have savings, so I still have time to decide what I want to do for a career.

"What's up?" I ask Jasper as I stop at a crosswalk.

"Not much. Evangeline is having a girl's night, so I thought that I would call and check in on you."

"I'm doing good. I just moved into my new apartment today, so I'm working on getting unpacked."

"You moved in with that girl, right?"

"Rae, yeah."

"How is she?" he asks.

"Good. I don't know her super well but she seems cool."

That wasn't entirely a lie. I don't know Rae as well as I would like to and she does seem cool. I want to tell Jasper that I want her, that I'm trying to think of how to ask her out without making things awkward between us.

"How's your shoulder and ribs?" he asks me.

"It's getting better. Training has been helping me get more strength back."

"That's good."

I know that Jasper gets it better than most. We were both injured while overseas and spent some time at the base in Germany healing before we came back to the States. Jasper hurt his shoulder too and it's been nice to have someone to talk to that is going through the same shitty thing as you.

"I was thinking about coming up for a few days to see Niall, you, and Ender," Jasper says as I cross the road.

"Yeah? I'm actually on my way to see Ender right now. We're going to grab a beer."

"Tell him I said hi and I'll see him in a few weeks."

"Do you have dates yet?" I ask him as I see the bar sign up ahead.

"I'm thinking the twentieth to the twenty-seventh."

"Okay, let me know when you get your ticket and I can pick you up."

"Will do."

"I'm at the bar now, but I'll talk to you in a few days."

"Sounds good."

We hang up and I head inside the bar. Ender is already there and I head over to join him. Ender has already ordered me a beer and I clap him on the back as I take the stool next to him.

"Have you been waiting long?" I ask him, and he shakes his head.

"Nah, I just got off work and walked in to order before you got here."

"How was work?"

He shrugs, taking a drink of his own beer.

"How was the move?"

I shrug back and he grins.

"I just talked to Jasper. He said he's thinking about coming up here at the end of the month for a week or so."

"Cool. Is he staying with you?"

"Probably his brother, but I didn't ask."

Ender nods again and I take a drink.

"How's Rae?"

Ender has always been able to read people better than most, so when he asks me that, I wonder if he knows how attracted I am to her or if he's just being polite.

"She's good."

He studies me as he raises his bottle to his lips and I look around the bar.

It's a hole in the wall place with wooden floors and brick walls. It's only about halfway filled with people but it's clean and the service seems fast.

Ender is still staring at me and I sigh.

"Yeah, so I'm into Rae."

"I know. Every time we've hung out as a group, you can't stop looking at her."

I wonder if she's noticed.

Do I want her to or not?

"It's funny though because you look at her and she looks away and then when you look away, she looks at you. You just never seem to look at each other at the same time."

I'm not sure what to make of that, so I stay silent and pick at the label on my beer bottle.

"Why don't you ask her out?" he asks when I stay silent.

"I just moved in with her. What if she says no or we do go out and it's a train wreck? Plus, I'm like a decade older than her. She's got her whole life ahead of her."

"And you, at twenty-nine, are washed up?" he asks me sarcastically and I roll my eyes.

"I just mean that we're at different points in our lives. I doubt that she would say yes if I asked her out, and I don't want to make things weird."

"Do you really think that that's going to happen?" he asks me and I pause.

"I don't know."

He nods and then changes the subject. He knows me well enough to know that I don't take unnecessary risks. Not since I joined the military and definitely not after the accident.

"How's training going? Are we going to be going to your fights soon?"

"No, I'll leave that to Niall, Finn, and Jameson."

Ender grins and I roll my eyes.

"How's the side?" he asks, nodding to my left side.

"It's getting there."

We start to talk about him and his fiancée, Cat. He's head over heels in love with her and I'm happy for him. I'm glad that all of my friends are happy and in love but it makes me feel like everyone is settled, except me.

I think about Rae again. She's so beautiful. She's got curves for days and this big, beautiful smile. She's my opposite in a lot of ways. I've got dark hair and she's got platinum blonde. My eyes are light blue and hers are a dark hazel color. She's bubbly and makes friends easily, whereas I'm more reserved.

"I was going to go volunteer at the veteran's hospital on Saturday. Think that you'd want to come with me?"

"I didn't know that you volunteered there," I say as I turn to him.

"I just started. I wanted to give back in some way and they have a new program where you can help as they train service dogs."

"Sure, I'm in. What time?"

We make plans to meet on Saturday and order another round of beers. He tells me about the tattoos that he did that day and I tell him about working out at the gym.

By the time that we leave, my shoulder is killing me and I know that I'm going to have to go home and ice it.

"I'll see you Saturday," Ender says as he heads over to his car.

I wave goodbye and start to walk home. The apartment is only a couple of blocks away and it's a nice night. The walk helps me clear my head and as I let myself into the apartment, I'm ready to shower and fall into bed.

Then I walk past the couch and see Rae curled up on it. The TV is still on and I lean over, turning it off before I go back and scoop her up in my arms.

My shoulder protests but I can't leave her sleeping like that. She'll wake up with a sore neck.

She smells like oranges and paper and I take a deep breath as I head into her room and gently lay her down on the bed.

She sighs as her head hits the pillow and then rolls over on her side. I smile as I cover her up and take one last look at her before I head down the hall to my own room.

I take a quick shower, dig through the boxes in my room until I find my own pajamas, and grab an ice pack from the freezer before I lay down in bed.

As I close my eyes, I swear that I can still smell Rae and I smile as I let sleep claim me.

THREE

Rae

I'M SO LATE.

I forgot to set my alarm before bed last night and when I woke up this morning, I spent way too much time wondering how I got to bed. I know that Brooks must have carried me in here and tucked me in, and I may have internally squealed at that thought before I turned and saw the time.

"Crap, crap, crap," I mumble as I throw on the first clean clothes that I can find, grab my backpack, and rush out of my bedroom.

I can hear Brooks moving around in his room and I want to tell him thanks for last night, but I don't have time.

I grab my keys and a granola bar and run out the door. When I make it down the stairs and outside, I groan.

I had parked on the street when I got home yesterday when there was no one else there but now there's a car behind me and in front of me. They're both about an inch from my bumper and I know that there's no way that I'll be able to get out.

"Shit," I sigh, looking up at the sky.

It's an overcast day and that seems fitting now.

There's no way that I'll be able to make it to campus in time for my first class now and I turn around to head back inside when I run right into Brooks.

"Whoa," he says, reaching out to steady me as I take a shaky step back.

"Sorry, I didn't see you there."

"Is everything okay?" he asks me, letting go of my elbow.

"Yeah, well, no actually. I'm running late and I'm parked in," I say, pointing over to my poor car.

Brooks looks over and frowns.

"I'll give you a ride," he says, turning and heading to the parking lot around the corner.

"Are you sure?"

"Yeah, I'm headed to King's Gym anyway."

I trail after him over to a newer model Camaro and climb into the passenger side while he puts his gym bag in the trunk.

"Where to?" he asks as he starts the car and backs out of his parking spot.

"Campus. I'll give you directions to the building."

He nods and we fall silent for a minute. This is already the longest that I've ever been alone with Brooks and I'm not sure what to say.

"Thanks for carrying me to bed last night. You didn't have to do that."

"It was no big deal," he says and I nod, looking away from him.

I don't last long though and soon I'm back to staring at him out of the corner of my eye. His hands are strong and capable on the steering wheel as he guides us through the early morning traffic.

"How's your shoulder?" I ask and I swear that he almost rolls his eyes.

"It's fine," he says shortly and it's kind of cute how annoyed he gets by that question.

"Sick of answering that question?" I ask with a smile.

"Yeah, it's getting a little old," he admits.

I want to ask him about the accident, but I get the feeling that he doesn't want to talk about it and definitely not with a girl that he barely knows.

"Maybe you shouldn't have carried me to bed," I start.

I'm not a small girl and I'm sure that my size sixteen butt was a little too much for his shoulder, especially after he was moving his things around all day.

"I'm fine. You're not heavy at all."

My insides warm at his words. I've always been a little self-conscious about my size but it's nice to know that Brooks doesn't care.

"Turn here," I tell him as he turns onto campus.

We wind down the street for a bit, stopping at a stop sign, and Brooks clears his throat.

"What are you studying?" he asks me, and I point out the next turn before I answer him.

"Physical therapy."

"Really? That's cool," he says as he pulls to a stop in front of my building.

I'm not surprised or offended that he was shocked to learn my major. I think most people expect me to say something a little more girly, but I've always wanted to be a physical therapist.

"Did you grow up in Pittsburgh?" he asks as I start to gather my backpack.

"No, I was in Philadelphia, but I wanted a change of pace."

"I bet your parents miss having you close," he says and I frown.

"I'm not so sure," I murmur.

I think that my mom misses having complete control over me more than she misses my company. Can I tell him that though? Do I even want to? My relationship with my mother is strained at best. We have a shaky understanding that I barely get, so explaining it to someone else seems hopeless.

"What about you? Where are you from?" I ask, trying to change the subject.

"I was born in Charleston, but I've been all over."

"You don't want to go back to the south?"

"Nah, I don't miss the heat and all of my family is scattered, so there's not much there for me."

I nod, getting ready to open the door, but I don't want to leave. Not now that we're actually talking and getting to know each other more.

"What was your favorite place?" I ask and he looks out the window at the dark clouds overhead for a moment as he thinks over my question.

"I'm liking Pittsburgh," he murmurs and my heart starts to beat faster.

Is it because of me? Am I reading too much into his words?

Probably.

"Thanks for the ride," I say as raindrops start to land on the windshield.

"No problem. Do you want me to come get you after class?"

"You don't have to. Palmer is on campus today, so I'll just get a ride back with her."

"It's no problem. I'm only a few blocks away."

I bite my bottom lip. Is it a good sign that he wants to pick me up? Or is he just being nice since we're roommates?

"Give me your phone number and you can text me once you decide," he tells me as it starts to rain harder.

I pass him my phone and watch as he enters his own number in.

"There," he says as he passes it back to me.

"Thanks. I'll see you later," I say, and he nods.

I jog up the sidewalk and into the building, shaking off the rain on me as I head down the hallway and into my class.

I make it just in time and I grab my laptop and try to pay attention to the lesson. It's no use though. All I can think about is Brooks and the car ride.

FOUR

Brooks

"HOW'S THE NEW PLACE?" Finn asks me as he joins me at the punching bags.

"It's good. I'm still unpacking and putting everything away but it's literally an exact copy of the room I had at Banks's."

He nods, stretching out his shoulders before he starts to hit his own bag.

"How's Sylvie?" I ask and Finn's whole body relaxes.

His girlfriend was in a car accident a few weeks ago and I know that she's recovered from it now. Finn still tends to hover around her though. Talking about Sylvie is the fastest way to get the guy to smile and I wonder if Rae has that effect on me.

"She's good. She just landed this big account at work so we're going out to celebrate tonight."

I met Finn, Niall, and Jameson when I started training at King's Gym. They're all good guys, but they're here to train to fight professionally and I'm just here to get stronger. Even though we're here for different reasons, we've still grown close over the last few months. I've been to see all of their fights and I've even sparred with them on occasion.

I've also watched all of them find their other half and settle down with them. I remember, before my attack, that I wanted that too. Being deployed didn't offer me a lot of time to find someone special and to be honest, every time that I went out to bars or clubs, no one ever piqued my interest.

Then that IED exploded and sent my life into a tailspin.

It had been a usual Monday morning and I was out on patrol with some guys from my unit. I remember us laughing at something that Rizzo said and then the sound of the explosion hit me.

It's strange, but the only thing that's stuck with me from that moment is the feel of the sand on my skin and the pain in my left side. My blood had felt cold and I remember thinking how weird that was as some guys from the convoy pulled me away from the wreckage.

I don't really remember much more than that, which the therapists that I saw all assured me was natural. My brain was trying to protect me so that I didn't relive it over and over. So that I didn't see all of my friends die.

I didn't care about falling in love when I was lying in that hospital bed in Germany or when I was going through physical therapy back in the States. Finding someone to settle down with wasn't even on my radar.

Until I met Rae.

Now I want what all of my friends have.

I haven't been able to stop thinking about Rae since the first time that I met her. I've gone out with my friends on outings solely to see and spend more time with her. When

Banks first came to me to ask if I would be willing to swap apartments so that Palmer could move in with him, I had jumped on it.

I wanted to spend as much time with Rae as I can. I was hoping that if she spent more time with me, maybe she would start to have feelings for me. The car ride this morning seemed promising but I feel like I never say the right thing around her.

I should have told her that she was beautiful or that I can't stop thinking about her. I should have asked her out on a date or canceled my plans with Ender last night so that I could have had pizza with her.

Now that I'm living with her, the temptation to make her mine is even stronger.

If she calls me for a ride home, then I'll ask her out. I spend the rest of my workout praying for my phone to ring.

I'm walking out of King's Gym and waving goodbye to Finn when my phone rings and I hurry to pull it out of my pocket. It's still pouring outside, so I hurry over to my car before I answer it.

"Hello?"

"Hey, Brooks. It's Rae. Palmer is staying late today for a group project. Do you think that you could come pick me up?" she asks, her sweet voice sounding worried and I can picture her pacing as she talks to me.

"Of course. I actually just left the gym, so I'll be there in ten. Which building are you in?"

"I'll meet you back by where you dropped me off. I'm only a few buildings away."

"See you soon."

"Thanks, Brooks."

I smile, trying to play out what I'll say to her as I drive through downtown and turn onto campus. Maybe I should wait until we get home. We could have dinner and I could ask her if she wanted to go out and grab a bite to eat with me tomorrow.

I pull up to the building that I dropped her off at this morning and see her running through the rain toward me. I hop out, running around to open her door for her, and she smiles at me as she slips past me.

"You didn't have to get out," she tells me as I climb back behind the wheel.

"Let me be a gentleman," I tell her as I head toward our apartment building.

I can see her smiling out of the corner of my eye and I relax.

"How was your day?" I ask her as we head home.

"Good. Long."

"Something wrong with your classes?"

"No, they were just dull today. I'm looking forward to going home and taking a hot shower and then relaxing for the rest of the night."

"Want to order burgers or something for dinner?" I ask as I pull up in front of the apartment.

"That sounds good," she says with a smile as she gathers her backpack.

"I'll drop you off here," I tell her and she smiles gratefully before she climbs out and heads inside the building.

I circle the block and park back in the parking lot on the side of our building before I run through the rain and inside.

I can hear the shower running as I come inside and I smile. That gives me a little more time to plan out how I'm going to ask her out.

"Hey, Rae?" I call as I knock on the bathroom door. "Did you want me to order the food now?"

The door opens a minute later and my mouth drops

open as I see Rae standing there soaking wet with a towel wrapped around her lush curves.

"What?" she asks, her blonde hair dripping water onto her shoulders.

Yeah, what was I saying?

My mind blanked as soon as I saw her and now all I want to do is grab her and kiss her. When she licks her lips, her body swaying toward mine, I decide to throw caution to the wind for the first time in a long while.

I grab her and seal her mouth with mine.

FIVE

Rae

IT FEELS SO right to be in Brooks's arms, with his mouth on mine. He grabs my hips, dragging me closer to him, and I can feel the towel starting to slip between us. I can't seem to find it in me to care though.

We stumble back, running into the wall next to my bedroom door and my belly flutters.

Are we going to do this? Do I want to have sex with him?

YES! my brain screams instantly.

I moan as Brooks's teeth nip at my bottom lip and he pulls back, staring into my eyes for a beat.

"I want you," he pants and I nod.

"I want you too," I admit and then we're back to making out.

Our lips connect and I open up for him, moaning into his mouth as he slides his tongue against mine. Brooks slides his hands down my body, stopping to cup my breasts when the towel eventually falls and lands at our feet before continuing his teasing touches down my body and gripping my hips.

I can't stop myself from lifting my hands to his chest and fisting his shirt, twisting the material in my fingers so hard that the buttons start to strain. Brooks grunts and cups my ass, pulling me closer to that thick bulge in his jeans. I can't stop myself from rocking against that hard ridge, desperate to ease the ache that's growing between my legs.

I'm rubbing against him, trying to get the friction I need, but it's not enough. Brooks groans, the vibrations tickling over my lips. I feel the muscles in his legs tense and flex beneath me, and I can't help but grind against him even harder.

"Rae," Brooks moans as I pull back to suck in some much-needed air and he starts to kiss his way down my neck.

Brooks's fingers grip my ass tighter, helping me grind against him harder and we both moan.

"Bed," I urge him and he nods against my shoulder.

His fingers wrap around mine and he tugs me behind him and into my bedroom. I turn to look at him and he pushes me down onto the bed.

I don't know why it didn't bother me when we were out in the hallway, but suddenly I'm self-conscious about being naked in front of him. When I look up though, his eyes are heated and he's devouring the sight of me laid out before him like a meal.

"Gorgeous."

I don't have time to respond or react before he's leaning over me, his lips claiming mine. My hands land on his shoulders and I fist the material of his shirt, wanting to feel his skin on mine.

Brooks reluctantly pulls away from me long enough to

tug his shirt off and throw it somewhere on my bedroom floor behind him. My eyes go to the scars that are now visible to me and I trace one finger around the one on his side. His eyes closed and I wonder if it's still painful for him to think about.

"I love your body," I whisper and he gives me a half smile.

When I tilt my face up, holding my hand up to him, he grins and we're back to that sexy place from before.

He falls down on top of me, caging me in with his arms as he kisses my neck, my jaw, my cheek, and finally, my lips.

We get lost touching, licking, and kissing each other for what feels like hours, but can only be minutes. When I come up for air, I realize that he is still partially dressed and that just won't do.

The ache in my core has only grown and now I'm desperate to feel him against me, inside me.

I push on his shoulders until he moves, kneeling between my legs, working on his belt and the button of his pants while I wiggle farther up the bed until I'm lying in the middle. I'm expecting him to crawl up my body and push inside of me, but instead, he grabs my ankles and pries my legs apart.

"Brooks," I start, but he's already settled between my legs and when he licks up my seam, whatever I was going to say gets cut off by my moan.

He growls and sucks on my clit, then lifts his head to look me in the eye. The sight of Brooks between my legs is really something to see. I almost come just from the way he's looking up at me, at the way his fingers are digging into my thighs, holding me open to him.

Brooks sucks on my clit and thrusts a finger inside of me

without warning. I cry out at the unexpected invasion, and then wiggle my hips, trying to get him to go deeper.

He leans back slightly so he can watch himself fuck me with his finger. The sloppy wet sounds fill the space and make me tremble in anticipation. I can't contain the whimper that spills out when he adds a second finger. I'm close, so, so close...

Brooks's eyes rise to meet mine. He looks at me like I'm the best thing that's ever happened to him. Like I'm the best thing that he's ever seen in his life.

I slam my eyes shut as a delicious wave of ecstasy sweeps through my body and rattles my bones.

"That's it, Rae," he whispers against my drenched core.

Then there's no more talking as he sucks on my clit in time with the thrusts of his fingers.

I hold my breath as my muscles draw up tight. For a moment I'm suspended in empty space, hovering, flying. The hard, merciless rhythm of his tongue is almost painful on my clit, overwhelming in the most glorious way. He twists his fingers and curls them up, breaking the tension over my body as the first wave of my orgasm floods through me.

I bow my back off of the mattress and cry out. I should probably be worried about the neighbors or anyone outside hearing us, but I can't. Not with my legs slamming shut against his head, trapping him there. Not with Brooks sliding his hands under my ass and squeezing the soft flesh. Hard.

I buck against his mouth as my release drips out of me.

The orgasm quickly rips through my body, leaving me breathless and unable to move once I come down from my high.

Brooks looks up at me from between my legs with unbridled lust. I don't stop to think about it, I just grab him, pull him up my body, and kiss him, tasting myself on his lips and moaning softly as he opens up for me.

I nibble on his lip and spread my legs wider for him, wanting more of his skin on my skin. Wanting to be connected to him in every single way. He settles his hips in between my legs, his hot and heavy cock laying across my slit.

He begins thrusting his hips, gliding his massive dick along my folds and gathering up my honey. My nerves sizzle and pop each time the head of his cock taps my swollen clit. I swear I could come just from this.

"Ready for me, baby?" Brooks whispers as he drags his cock through my slick folds.

I take a second to appreciate Brooks's beauty. The way his broad shoulders and strong arms roped with muscles strain as he holds himself above me, careful not to crush me. His defined pecs and abs flex for me as my eyes roam over his tanned skin. I allow myself a few more seconds of open gawking before trailing my gaze back up to meet his.

"God yes," I say as I tilt my hips up and try to take him into my body.

Brooks chuckles, dipping his head to kiss me as he lines up with my drenched hole.

The tip of his cock nudges into my entrance, only going in a fraction of an inch. Even so, my opening stretches to accommodate his size, a burning sensation tearing through my core and making my muscles tighten in protest.

"I've got you, Rae," he whispers against my lips before kissing me slowly. "I'm going to make this so fucking good for you."

He presses his forehead to mine and eases in another inch, then another.

"Stop teasing me," I moan, and I can feel him smile against my lips.

He kisses me as he thrusts into me fully. I let out a yelp, my muscles protesting his size and Brooks holds himself still, giving me time to adjust to the feel of him inside me.

"Oh my god, Brooks, fuck..." I moan, crossing my ankles behind his back in an attempt to keep him there, so deep inside of me.

"Rae," he chokes out like he's in pain.

He starts to move slowly, letting both of us find a rhythm. It's not long before he's grunting and snapping his hips against mine, pulling nearly all the way out and slamming home in one hard thrust. I choke on the scream in my throat and bow my back off of the bed, clawing at his back as he hammers in and out of me. Each time he hits the end of me, my body jerks as if being electrocuted.

"Don't... stop..." I breathe out as I cling to his big body.

"Not a fucking chance," he snarls, bending down to suck on one of my nipples.

His thrusts become harder, faster, as he licks and nips his way up to my mouth. His lips are inches from mine. All I can think about is tasting him while he fucks me.

"Let go, Rae. I've got you. Come for me."

He kisses me as he slams into me in long, rough strokes. I'm stuffed so full of his cock that it feels like I can't take a full breath. I unhook my ankles from behind him and place my feet flat on the floor so I can meet him thrust for thrust.

"Christ, you feel incredible," he mumbles into the side of my neck.

I scream as my orgasm rips through me, all of my muscles spasming at once in the most intense moment I've ever experienced. My blood feels like sharp razor blades coursing through my veins, the pain spiking my pleasure into heights unknown.

I whimper and squeeze my walls around his hard length, unable to give him any words at the moment. My body is deliciously sore and used, my pussy is swollen and sensitive, and I don't think I can take anything else.

"*Fuck!*"

Brooks roars out his release as he sinks into me so deep, shooting his hot cum deep inside of me.

"You okay?" he whispers a few minutes later as we both lay sprawled across the bed.

"Uhhmm," I sigh unintelligibly, but Brooks seems to understand.

We lay there, a mess of tangled limbs and drying sweat, just breathing the same air and snuggling in the afterglow. I've always wanted a love like this, and who would have guessed it would be Brooks, my boss, that would be the one to give it to me?

"Hey, Rae?" he asks, his voice ragged and strained.

"Hmm?" I ask, my eyes falling closed.

"Will you go out to dinner with me tomorrow night?" he asks and I smile.

"Absolutely."

SIX

Brooks

EVEN THOUGH RAE and I slept together last night, tonight is still important. I need everything to go perfectly so that I can show Rae that we're meant to be together.

Sleeping with her last night only proved even more how perfect she is for me. It was incredible and I want to do it for the rest of my life. Waking up with her in my arms was literally a dream come true.

I check out my reflection one last time before I head out into the hallway. Rae is still in her room getting ready but she should be out soon. I put my shoes on and pocket my car keys before I peek a look down the hallway.

I can hear Rae moving around in her room, so I take a seat on the couch and go over the plans for tonight.

I'm going to take her out to dinner at this upscale place a few blocks from us and then for a walk along the river. We can end the night with a movie on the couch if she's not too tired.

The bedroom door opens and I leap to my feet. Rae rounds the corner and we both freeze as we stare at each other, taking everything in. It feels like the earth stops spinning as I look at Rae. I can feel in my gut that this moment is going to be important. Life changing, even.

"You look incredible," I tell her and she smiles as she walks over to my side.

"Thanks. So do you."

"Are you ready to go?" I ask her, and she nods, tucking a little clutch purse beneath her arm.

I take her hand in mine as we head out of the apartment and down to my car.

"It's so nice out," Rae says and I nod.

"Did you want to walk? The restaurant is only three blocks away."

"Sure, I could stretch my legs after sitting in class all day."

I shove my keys back in my pocket and we start to walk down the sidewalk. The sidewalks are mostly empty since everyone has already headed home.

"How was class today?" I ask her and she starts to tell me about her day.

She's still a freshman, so she's taking all of her general study classes and getting them out of the way. I can tell that she's looking forward to when she gets into the classes that are for her actual major.

"Oh, I wanted to try this place," she says as we reach the restaurant and I open the door for us.

"Then I'm glad that I picked it."

We check in with the hostess and after following her through the restaurant, we are seated at our table by the window.

"Everything looks so good," Rae says as we browse the menu.

"Want to split a few things?" I ask and Rae nods.

We decide on a few appetizers, a couple of sides, and two entrees. Once the waiter has taken our order, the conversation turns to my day.

"I just went to King's Gym and then grabbed lunch with Ender," I tell her. "I'm going to the VA Hospital with him tomorrow to volunteer with some wounded vets."

"Really? That's so cool!"

She tells me about how she used to volunteer at the animal shelter back in Philadelphia before the conversation turns back to me and the military.

"What made you enlist?" she asks as our appetizers are set in front of us.

"I didn't know what I wanted to do after high school. I wanted to see the world and there weren't really any jobs in my town, so when the army recruiter approached me, I signed up."

"Did you like it? Before the accident, I mean," she hurries to add.

"It was okay. I liked the routine and feeling like I was making a difference or being part of a team. A lot of the guys in my unit were cool."

We polish off one of the appetizers and I let Rae take the first bite of the goat cheese and tomato confit before I grab my own.

"So you don't miss it then?"

I have to think about her question.

"Sometimes. Or I guess I miss some aspects. It's hard for me to not know what I want to do with my life. I don't like not having a plan. I don't miss the desert and all of the orders though."

"Can I ask... how did you hurt your shoulder and side?" she asks and I knew that this question was coming.

"It was an IED. We were out on patrol and my Humvee got hit."

"I'm so sorry."

"There was a Humvee behind ours and those guys pulled me out but it was too late for the rest of the guys."

"Brooks, I'm so sorry," Rae says with tears in her hazel eyes and I clear my throat.

"Thanks."

The waiter comes back and clears the plates away before our entrees and sides are set down and it gives us a moment to get back to more neutral territory.

"What about you? Have you ever been anywhere cool?" I ask her as we divide up the food.

"Not really. My mom didn't like leaving Philadelphia. I want to travel though. Maybe after I've graduated."

We talk about places that we want to see as we eat and I'm pleased to know that we have a lot of the same interests.

"Do you want dessert?" I ask and Rae leans back in her chair.

"Oh no. I'm so stuffed," she says with a sigh and I nod.

I pay the bill and we head out.

"Want to walk back along the river?" I ask and she nods, so I take her hand and we head that way.

The sun has set and the moon is out. It's a perfect night and I'm glad that the weather held for our date.

"This was the best first date," Rae says as we near our building. "Well, it was actually my first first date."

"Mine too," I tell her with a smile.

"Really? How is that possible?" she asks as I open our apartment door.

"I was always deploying. It wasn't great for meeting

new people or starting a relationship. And no one ever caught my eye. Not until you."

I shut the door and when I turn around, Rae jumps me.

Her lips land on mine and my hands grip her hips and hold her to me.

Rae pulls back far too soon and my lips chase after hers. I wasn't done with her mouth yet but when she whispers against my mouth, "I want to taste you," all thoughts of kissing her go out of my head.

"What?"

"I want to taste you. Like you tasted me last night."

I can only nod as she takes a step back and then she's sinking to her knees before me. Her fingers fumble with my dress pants and my mouth starts to dry as I watch her. All of the blood in my brain is heading south to my cock and by the time she pulls my cock out of my underwear, I'm close to coming.

She glances up at me, her hazel eyes full of desire and my knees go weak. By the time that she wraps her hand around me and is swallowing the tip between her plump lips, I'm feeling dizzy with lust.

"Rae," I start but then she swallows another inch and all thoughts leave my head.

Her hand starts to move up and down my length and my hand lands on the doorknob to try to steady myself.

"Rae, I'm going to come," I grit out through clenched teeth.

I don't want to come in her mouth if she doesn't want me to, but it's getting harder to hold back my release.

Rae moans and the vibrations send shivers down my spine.

"Rae," I groan as my balls tighten up and I start to come.

Rae swallows me all down and I go limp against the

door.

"How was that?" she asks and I reach down to help her to her feet.

"Mind blowing," I say before I pull her against me and kiss her.

She lifts her arms as I move to tug her dress up and over her head. I race to get her naked as soon as possible and then I'm spinning us, kicking off my own clothes, and then lifting her into my arms and pinning her against the door.

"Ready for me, baby?" I ask and she nods eagerly.

I reach between us, testing her opening to make sure that she's wet enough for me. She's drenched and I smile as I guide my cock to her opening and thrust inside.

"Brooks," she moans and I pick up my pace.

We're both chasing our peaks and I'm determined to make her come first. Her tits bounce in my face and I reach up, dragging down the cup of her bra so that I can suck her nipple into my mouth.

Rae screams and I fuck into her harder, faster. I can feel my own orgasm starting to build inside of me.

"Come for me, baby," I order and she screams my name as her juices flood my cock.

Thank god.

I chant her name as I find my own release.

We both catch our breath and I slowly let her slide down to her feet. Once I know that she's steady on her feet, I take a step back.

"Can we do that again?" Rae asks after a beat and I grin at her.

"As many times as you want," I tell her, and she squeals as she jumps into my arms.

I catch her easily and carry her into my bedroom for round two.

SEVEN

Rae

SE7EN IS PACKED the next night I work and I paste on a smile as I elbow my way through the crowd. I should be used to it by now since I've been working at this club for the last few months.

Maybe I'm just antsy because Brooks is here tonight. We haven't gotten to spend much time together since our date the other night because I've been at work.

He still sleeps in my bed every night, but I get home so late that we haven't done anything but sleep since our date.

I miss seeing him during the day though and I'm getting tired of the only time we spend together being when we're sleeping.

"It's crazy in here," Palmer says as she joins me at the side of the bar.

We're both loading up our trays and I take a deep breath, looking out over the crowd. I haven't seen Brooks yet but he texted me when I got here saying that he was going to come see me. I told him when I usually take my breaks, but now, I'm wondering if it's going to get pushed back until the crowd dies down a bit.

"Looking for Brooks?" Palmer asks me, giving me a grin as she adds glasses to her tray.

I told her about us sleeping together and going out together and she's been our biggest cheerleader so far. I think that she's just happy that I've found someone too. It doesn't hurt that she already knows and likes Brooks.

"Yeah, I haven't seen him yet," I admit.

"That's not surprising. I haven't seen him yet either, but I'll keep an eye out for him."

I smile at her as she hefts her tray and heads back out into the crowd. I finish loading my own tray and take one last look around the bar for Brooks before I head over to the VIP section.

I pass out bottles and drinks, still keeping an eye out for him but as I head back to the bar for another round of drinks, I catch sight of his dark hair.

I smile, already turning and heading in that direction when the crowd parts and I see some girl hanging off of him.

My heart sinks and I freeze in my tracks.

It could be that she just bumped into him, or maybe they know each other, but then why isn't he pushing her away? Why are they standing so close? Why is he letting her touch him like that?

I spin away from the scene and head back to the bar. I'm breathing hard and I can feel unshed tears stinging my eyes.

"I'll be right back," I tell one of the bartenders and they nod, giving me a concerned look but I'm already pushing into the back and trying to get myself under control.

I head into the empty break room and lean against the wall.

I know in my heart that Brooks isn't into her and he's not cheating on me. I know that this is all of my mom's bullshit and hang-ups and that I shouldn't doubt him. He hasn't given me any real reason to doubt him and yet I can't stop turning what I saw out in the club into something more sinister.

"There you are! Brooks is here and..." Palmer trails off as she catches sight of my face and I try to smile but it feels more like a wince.

"I saw him," I say quietly and she rushes to my side.

"What happened? What's wrong?"

"He was with some other girl."

"He kissed her?! I'm going to kill him!" Palmer says and I stop her.

"No, he... I'm going to sound crazy. She was just hanging off of him, but he wasn't pushing her away."

"And you immediately thought of your mom and dad," she finishes and I nod. "He wasn't doing anything bad," she says kindly and I nod again.

"I know. I just need to get it straight in my head."

"What can I do?" she asks as she squeezes my shoulder.

"Nothing. I know that it's my mom's voice in my head. I just need to get her to shut up," I joke with a halfhearted smile.

"Okay. Let me know if I can do anything," she says and I nod.

She gives my hand a squeeze before she turns and heads back out to work. I know that I need to follow her but I just need to get myself under control a little more.

Even though I know that this is all in my head, I can't seem to stop the doubt from flooding in.

What even are Brooks and I? We've slept together twice and gone out on one date so it's not like we're exclusive.

Maybe I was just building this up to be something big in my head, or maybe I'm taking things more seriously than Brooks is.

I wipe my eyes, taking a few deep breaths and pushing out the door to the club. I know that I'm going to see Brooks and I'll have to talk to him, but I don't know what I'll say to him or how I'll react.

I manage to get through delivering another round of drinks before I come face to face with Brooks. He grins when he catches my eye, obviously happy to see me, but I don't know what I feel as he comes my way.

"Hey! There you are!" he yells over the music as he stops at my side.

I give him a small smile but it feels forced.

"Hey," I say back, my voice lacking any emotion.

"Are you alright?" he asks, his brow wrinkling in concern.

"Yeah, I'm just tired. It's been a busy night."

He nods in sympathy and rubs my shoulders.

"Can you take a break soon?"

"Sorry, I think that it will be a while," I tell him and he frowns.

"Damn. Well, my friend Jasper decided to come into town. He was supposed to be here next week but he moved it up a week, so I'm actually headed to pick him up from the airport. I'll see you at home though, okay? I'll rub your feet or maybe we can take a bath," he says with a sexy smirk and I nod.

"I'll see you later," I tell him, and he kisses me quickly before he's heading for the door.

I watch him go, wondering what I'm going to do when I go home tonight.

I need to get past this. I just don't know how.

EIGHT

Brooks

I DON'T KNOW where I messed up with Rae.

Things had been going along so well, or so I thought. Then Jasper came to town and everything seemed to go off the rails.

I thought maybe she was trying to give me space so that I could see my friend, but it's more than that. She's been distant since I saw her at Se7en. Maybe even before that since we weren't seeing each other a ton.

Her mom flew in for a visit today so it looks like I'll have to wait until she leaves to ask her what's going on.

Part of me was hoping that Rae would ask me to meet her mom, but she didn't. I get the feeling that there's a weird dynamic between the two based off of comments that she's made in passing but I never asked her. She made it seem like she didn't want to talk about it and I didn't want to rock the boat. Now I'm left wondering if her mom's visit is what has her acting weird.

I climb the stairs to our apartment and let myself in. The place is empty and I sigh as I head into my room. I left the gym early, hoping to catch Rae before she left to get her mom from the airport but I guess I was too late.

She should be home soon though. Maybe I can offer to make everyone dinner.

I pull my phone out, intending on calling Rae to see what the plan is for tonight when I hear the front door open.

"I still think that you should have lived on campus in the dorms," comes a prim voice and I know that it must be Rae's mother.

"I'm safe here too, Mom."

"Not while you're living with that man," her mom says, her voice filled with disgust and I wonder why she seems to hate me so much.

"Brooks is a really nice guy."

Her mom hums and I hear them walk past my bedroom and into Rae's room.

"Your room is small."

"It's fine for me."

"You should have your desk over there. You'd get more light that way and wouldn't be causing your eyes so much strain."

"I'll move it later," Rae says and she sounds so worn down that it has my fingers curling into fists.

"Is his room bigger?" her mom asks, the disdain clear in her voice.

"No, Mom. They're identical rooms and sizes."

"Wouldn't you rather live with a woman?"

Does Rae not like living with me?

"I like living with Brooks, Mom."

There's a pause and I relax at her words.

"Are you dating him?"

I swear that my heart stops beating as I wait to hear what Rae's answer is. I hold my breath, my body moving on its own accord so that I'm closer to the wall that's separating us.

"Mom," she starts, sounding defeated.

I hate hearing her sound like that and I wonder why her mom has so much power over her.

"You are! I thought that I raised you better than that, Rae Anne."

"Mom," she starts again, but the woman seems to be on a roll.

"You'll learn that he'll just leave or cheat on you. He's a man. They can't help it," she seethes and I wonder what happened between her parents to cause her mom to hate all men, sight unseen.

Rae is silent and I assume that she's used to this anti-men bullshit, but apparently her mom sees something different.

"Oh... he already has, hasn't he?" her mom says, her voice dropping from the shout that it was before.

"No, I mean, I don't know, but I want to trust him."

My heart stops beating at her words.

What does she mean, she doesn't know? Why can't she trust me? When have I ever given her a reason to think that she is not the center of my whole fucking world?

I'm moving before I realize that I gave my body a command. If Rae doesn't know how obsessed I am with her, then I've been doing something wrong.

I'm done holding myself back with her. She should never doubt how much she means to me, how much I love her.

I burst into Rae's room, my eyes finding her immediately.

"Why can't you trust me?" I blurt out and Rae looks between me and her mom, her hazel eyes wide.

"The club, Seven. I saw some girl hanging off of you."

I frown, trying to remember any girl at the club but come up blank.

"Who? I don't remember that."

"I saw her hanging off of you. You were letting her."

"Of course, he was," her mom says, crossing her arms over her chest. "He's what? Ten years older than you? Why do you think a man like that wants a pretty young girl like you? You're nothing to him."

"That's not true. At all," I argue and I can see her mom throw her arms up in the air in annoyance out of the corner of my eye.

"Yeah, I am close to a decade older than Rae, but that's never bothered me. Rae is so smart and mature. She gets me, and I get her."

Her mom huffs at that, and I spare her a glance and see that she looks just as bitter and miserable as she sounds. Her hair is pulled back into a severe bun and her mouth is pinched. It makes me wonder when the last time that she smiled was.

"I don't know who she was. I don't even remember her. I went there to see you. I'm *obsessed* with you," I stress and Rae bites her bottom lip.

She still seems uncertain and so I take a step toward her, taking her hands in mine.

"I've never wanted anyone else, Rae, and I never will. I swear. You're the only one for me."

I stare into her hazel eyes, trying to get her to see just how much she means to me. I can see her softening and her mom must see it too because she tries to get between us.

"Leave my daughter alone!" she snaps at me but I just keep staring at Rae.

"I love you, Rae. Don't let her put lies in your head," I beg her.

"Get out! And I think that it's best that you find another place to live."

"No," Rae says, her voice barely a whisper, but we both hear it and turn to look at her.

"What did you say, young lady?"

"I said no. He's not moving out."

"Maybe you should be the one to move out then. Your old room is still the way that you left it. You can come home and go to a school closer to me."

"No, Mom. I like it here. I like my classes and my friends and I really like Brooks. I shouldn't have let you get in my head. You had me doubting the best thing that's ever happened to me," she says before she turns and gives me a soft smile.

My heart rate should be calming down now that I know that she's not going to leave or break up with me, but instead it starts to race again.

Does she mean me? Could she be in love with me too?

NINE

Rae

I CAN'T BELIEVE that I almost let my mother get in my head and cause me to lose Brooks. I was being ridiculous thinking that he would ever cheat on me. He's been a complete gentleman since we met, and I know that he would never do anything to hurt me.

I should have been more mature and just talked to him when I saw him at the club. I should have told off my mom a long time ago.

As I watched her try to run off Brooks, I had a vision of what my life would be like if I let my mother have her way. I would be bitter and all alone, or worse, resentful and still living with her.

That's not the life that I want and I know that I need to change if I don't want it to be my future.

"Mom, I think that maybe you should leave," I tell her without taking my eyes off of Brooks.

I know without looking that her face is red with anger,

her eyes spitting fire at me as she glares at me. I've never pushed her away before. She's always done it first. I've never really stood up to her either.

Brooks has given me the courage to go after the life that I want. He's given me a reason to chase my own happiness instead of doing what my mother dictates or thinks is best.

"Can I talk to you for a minute, Rae? In private," she stresses before she storms out of the room.

"I should deal with her," I say but I don't really want to face her alone.

My newfound independence still seems so shaky and I know how cutting she can be.

"I'll go with you," Brooks tells me, kissing the top of my head before he takes my hand.

I'm relieved that he could see how nervous I was and is going to have my back here.

"I said alone," my mother snaps and Brooks squeezes my hand, urging me to be strong.

"I want him here."

I can tell that she wants to say something about that, but she bites her tongue. Her glare turns glacier and I take a step closer to Brooks, relying on his support to get through this.

"You should come home. It's obvious that the people here aren't having a positive influence on you."

"Why is that? Because I'm not jumping at your every command?" I ask.

"You don't backtalk me, young lady!" she snaps, and I grit my teeth.

"This is my home. I'm an adult now. You can't expect me to respect you if you don't show me and my boyfriend respect. I want you to leave, but before you do, you need to understand that I'm not your little puppet anymore. I'm going to live my life the way that I want to and you need to get on board with that."

My mom looks at me for one full minute before she storms past me. She comes back with her suitcase and slams her way out of our apartment.

As soon as the door closes behind her, I'm in Brooks's arms.

"I'm sorry, Rae. She should be more supportive of you. We can get her to come around," he tries to reassure me as his hands stroke up and down my back.

"No, she won't."

He holds me tighter and I wrap my arms around his waist, letting him comfort me.

"Say it again," I whisper after a few minutes and Brooks tenses for a minute, trying to figure out what I'm asking of him.

Finally, he gets it and says the three words that I'm dying to hear.

"I love you."

I sigh, smiling for what feels like the first time in days.

"I love you too."

"Thank God. I was worried that you would think that it would be too fast."

"It is fast, but that doesn't change how I feel."

He smiles down at me and I wrap my arms around his neck, tipping my mouth up for his to claim.

I want to get lost in him and forget all about my messy relationship with my mom and everything that just happened. We just said I love you for the first time and I want to make love to my man now.

Brooks seems to get the message because his lips claim mine right away. I let him back me up to the couch and once we reach it, he pushes me down so that I'm lying on the soft cushions.

Our kisses turn slow as Brooks peels off our clothes, caressing my body as he goes.

"I love you, Rae," he says as he trails kisses down my stomach.

He settles between my legs and my response dies on my tongue as I watch him lick his lips and dip his head toward my core.

He makes love to me with his mouth and I get lost in the sensations, in the feeling of him worshipping my body. He makes me come with his tongue, and then his fingers, and it feels like I'm floating on a cloud as he finally kisses his way back up my body and thrusts into me in one languid move.

"I love you," I mumble against his lips and he smiles.

"I love you too."

Then I close my eyes and kiss him as he shows me just how much he does.

TEN

Brooks

ONE YEAR LATER...

I LOOK over at my wife as we sit sprawled out on the couch watching some romance movie that she picked out. Rae's eyes are locked on the screen and she's mouthing the words along with the characters.

She's adorable.

We've watched this movie at least a dozen times in the last year but I always watch Rae. She's so cute when she reacts to it that it's much more entertaining than any movie ever could be.

"Watch the movie," Rae chides as she kicks my leg with her foot.

I capture her foot and start rubbing it as I pretend to turn back to the screen.

Rae and I got married six months ago. It was actually a

month after Palmer and Banks got married. Palmer had been pushing for us to have a joint wedding but I wanted a day to celebrate just Rae and I.

Jasper and Evangeline flew in for the big day and ended up staying for a few days. It was nice to catch up with him again and to see him so happy with his own wife.

Her mother didn't come. Well, we actually didn't send her an invite. Rae and her haven't really talked since she stormed out of our place. I would say that it's a loss, but neither Rae nor I miss seeing her or having her be part of our life.

Rae did try to reach out to her about two weeks after she left. I sat by her side for the phone call, praying that it would go the way that Rae wanted. I think we both knew that it wasn't going to go that way though and it didn't.

I held her while she cried and did my best to console her. That was the last that we heard from her.

"You're not watching," Rae says again, a laugh in her voice.

"Sure, I am."

She rolls her eyes and I grin.

Rae is still in college. She has two years left before she gets her degree and we're trying to decide if we want to stay in Pittsburgh after that or travel somewhere new.

I started working at the VA Hospital a few months ago. I was volunteering with Ender every week and one day they offered me a job. I was happy to accept. Working and being around veterans, people who were going through what I went through, was never something that I had thought I would like before, but once I started going, I loved it.

Rae has even been volunteering with me on some weeks. She loves helping people and since we're working with the service dogs and training, she's been dying for us to get a dog. I don't want to ruin the surprise but I found us an adorable golden retriever, her favorite breed, a few days ago and I'm all set to go pick him up tomorrow.

"If you're not going to watch..." Rae starts and I grab her other foot and start to rub the sole.

We're still living next door to Palmer and Banks and we see them all the time. Rae and Palmer go out with Sylvie, Everly, and Phoenix for girl's nights at least once a month, and I get to hang out with the guys from King's Gym.

I don't get to see them as much now that they're big, famous boxers and I'm working during the day.

"That's it," Rae sighs, grabbing the remote and turning off the movie.

I look over at her, and she grins at me as she moves to straddle my lap.

"I think that we can find something else to hold your attention," she purrs against my mouth, and I grin.

I'm one lucky bastard, I think as her lips land on mine, and I get lost in the woman that I love.

ELEVEN

Rae

FIVE YEARS LATER...

I HURRY INTO THE APARTMENT, double checking that Brooks isn't home from the VA Hospital yet before I rush into our bedroom and straight into the bathroom. I dig out the pregnancy test that I bought at lunch and open it to read the instructions.

It seems pretty straightforward. I pee on the stick, setting it on the bathroom counter and pacing as I wait the three minutes for the results.

I had been feeling nauseous and so tired the last few weeks. I thought that maybe it was the flu, or I was coming down with something else, or maybe I was just working too much. Then I missed my period and realized that it could be something else entirely.

"Rae? You home, baby?" Brooks calls and I hear the front door close behind him.

"Yeah! Be out in a minute!" I call as I wring my hands together.

I still have a few more seconds before I can check the test and I hold my breath as I count down the seconds. Finally, my alarm goes off on my phone and I turn the test so that I can see it.

Two pink lines.

I let out a laugh as my heart starts to beat so loud that I can hear it in my ears.

"Rae? Are you okay?" Brooks asks, and I can tell that he's outside the bathroom door.

I open it, grinning at him, and he smiles back at me.

"Did you have a good day?" he asks as he pulls me into his arms.

"Yeah," I say, hugging him back as I grip the pregnancy test tighter in my hand. "How was your day?"

"Good. We made some progress with the group today," he says, and he sounds proud.

Brooks decided to go to college a few years ago and graduated with a psychology degree just a few months ago. He's been promoted at the VA Hospital and I'm so proud of him. He gets to do something that he loves, something that gives him a purpose and makes a difference in so many soldiers' lives.

"That's great!"

"Yeah, it's been a positive day," Brooks says as he pulls back and moves to take my hand.

"Yes, a very *positive* day." I giggle.

That's when he sees what I'm holding.

"Rae," he says, his voice cutting off as he looks back up at me for an answer.

"I'm pregnant," I say, my voice coming out hoarse as tears spring to my eyes.

"A baby?" he asks, his hands going to my stomach. "We're having a baby?"

"Yeah," I tell him, the tears slipping free and streaking down my cheeks.

Then I'm in Brooks's arms and I laugh as I wrap my arms around him.

"You're happy?" I ask and he chuckles.

"Of course. I love you, Rae. You're my whole world. I want a family with you. I want everything with you."

I squeeze him tighter, burying my face in his chest, and I can tell that he's smiling as he rubs my back.

I wasn't really worried about Brooks's reaction. He still treats me like I'm the center of his world and even though we agreed to wait until we were both done with college to have kids and were more settled in our careers, it feels like the time is right.

I started working for the Pittsburgh Penguins as one of the team's physical trainers. I wasn't much of a hockey fan before, but Brooks loves it and we've even gone to a few games together.

We're in the off season now, so work is pretty light and it couldn't be a better time for me to deal with the first trimester symptoms.

"Should you be sitting down?" Brooks asks and I laugh.

I knew that he was going to be overprotective as soon as he found out that I was pregnant and it looks like I was right.

"Maybe. I'm pretty tired," I admit as I yawn.

"Come on then. I'll tuck you in and make us some dinner."

I let my husband lead me into our bedroom and tuck me

into our bed. He kisses my forehead, giving me a smile before he heads out to the kitchen.

We're still in the same apartment that we fell in love in and as my eyes close, I wonder if we'll have to find a bigger place soon.

I don't care where we live. As long as I have my tempting man, I'll be happy and I know that Brooks feels the same.

I smile as I give in and fall asleep.

ARE *you curious about Banks and Palmer? Check out their book here here!*

ABOUT THE AUTHOR

CONNECT WITH ME!

If you enjoyed this story, please consider leaving a review on Amazon or any other reader site or blog that you like. Don't forget to recommend it to your other reader friends.

If you want to chat with me, please consider joining my VIP list or connecting with me on one of my Social Media platforms. I love talking with each of my readers. Links below!

Website
Newsletter

Cherry Falls

803 Wishing Lane

1012 Curvy Way

Eye Candy Ink

Atlas

Mischa

Sam

Zeke

Nico

Eye Candy Ink: Second Generation

Ames

Harvey

Rooney

Gray

Ender

Banks

Fallen Peak

A Very Mountain Man Valentine's Day

A Very Mountain Man Halloween

A Very Mountain Man Thanksgiving

A Very Mountain Man Christmas

A Very Mountain Man New Year

Folklore

Kidnapping His Forever

Claiming His Forever

Finding His Forever

Rescuing His Forever

Chasing His Forever

Folklore: The Complete Series

Holiday Hearts

Be Mine

Falling in Love

Holly Jolly Holidays

Love Notes

Signing Off With Love

Care Package Love

Wrong Number, Right Love

Kings Gym

Fighting Fire With Fire

Fighting Tooth and Nail

Fighting Back From Hell

Mine To

Mine to Love

Mine to Protect

Mine to Cherish

Mine to Keep

Mine to: The Complete Series

Sequoia: Stud Farm

Branded

Bucked

Roped

Spurred

Sequoia: Fast Love Racing

Jump Start

Pit Stop

Home Stretch

Telltale Heart

Bought and Paid For

His Miracle

Pretty Girl

Telltale Hearts Boxset

ALSO BY SHAW HART

Still in the mood for Christmas books?

Stuffing Her Stocking, Mistletoe Kisses, Snowed in For Christmas, Coming Down Her Chimney

Love holiday books? Check out these!

For Better or Worse, Riding His Broomstick, Thankful for His FAKE Girlfriend, His New Year Resolution, Hop Stuff, Taming Her Beast, Hungry For Dash, His Firework

Looking for some OTT love stories?

Her Scottish Savior, Baby Mama, Tempted By My Roommate, Blame It On The Rum, Wild Ride, Always

Looking for a celebrity love story?

Bedroom Eyes, Seducing Archer, Finding Their Rhythm

In the mood for some young love books?

Study Dates, His Forever, My Girl

Some other books by Shaw:

The Billionaire's Bet, Her Guardian Angel, Falling Again, Stealing Her, Dreamboat, Making Her His, Trouble

9 798223 866459